AFRICA IS MY HOME

A CHILD OF THE *AMISTAD*

MONICA EDINGER

illustrated by **ROBERT BYRD**

CANDLEWICK PRESS

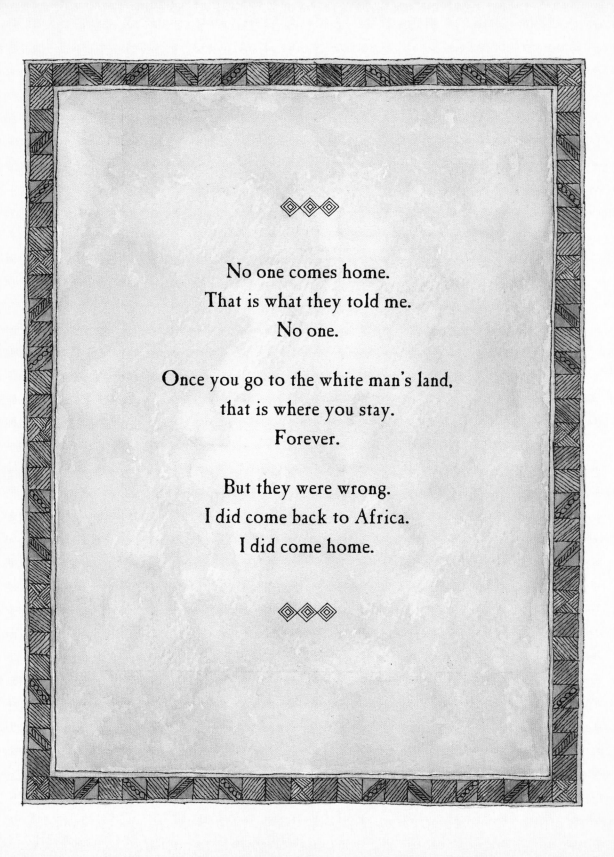

No one comes home.
That is what they told me.
No one.

Once you go to the white man's land,
that is where you stay.
Forever.

But they were wrong.
I did come back to Africa.
I did come home.

Europe

Asia

Mediterranean Sea

Algiers

Tripoli

Cairo
Egypt

Arabia

Red Sea

The Sahara

Dakar

Timbuktu

Khartoum
Sudan

West Africa

Addis Ababa
Ethiopia

Freetown
Mendeland

Mt. Kilimanjaro
Nairobi

Lake Victoria

Freetown

Gallinas River

Lomboko

The Congo

Coast of Mendeland

Madagascar

Transvaal

Atlantic Ocean

South Africa

Indian Ocean

Cape Town

N
W   E
S

· A F R I C A · 1839 ·

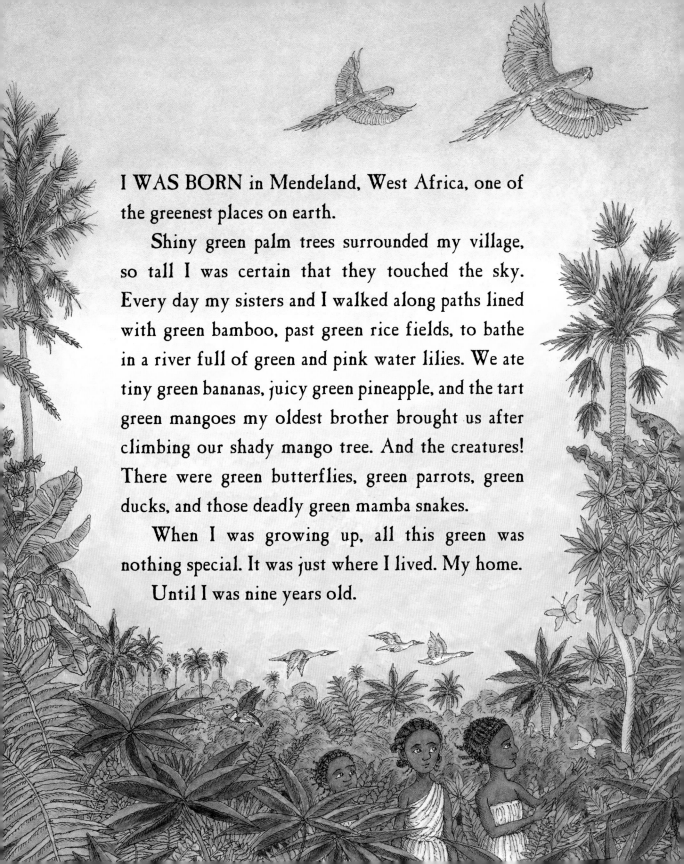

I WAS BORN in Mendeland, West Africa, one of the greenest places on earth.

Shiny green palm trees surrounded my village, so tall I was certain that they touched the sky. Every day my sisters and I walked along paths lined with green bamboo, past green rice fields, to bathe in a river full of green and pink water lilies. We ate tiny green bananas, juicy green pineapple, and the tart green mangoes my oldest brother brought us after climbing our shady mango tree. And the creatures! There were green butterflies, green parrots, green ducks, and those deadly green mamba snakes.

When I was growing up, all this green was nothing special. It was just where I lived. My home.

Until I was nine years old.

It was a bad time; I remember that.

The rice was long gone, the mango tree empty, and we had nothing. The littlest children were listless from hunger, their bellies bloated in emptiness. Our elders could barely move. We ate leaves, bark, anything we could find. Two babies had already died, and we feared that more would before the rains began.

"Daughter," my father said, "there is a man in our village. He has rice to give us on one condition: that you go to him as pawn. You will work for his family — fetch water, care for his children, help with the cooking — whatever they need you to do. At the next harvest, I will return what I owe and you will come home. So it has to be."

Yes, so it had to be. More would die otherwise. The harvest wasn't that far off; I could bear being away from home till then. But then the slave traders saw me and the man became greedy. My father begged and pleaded for more time, but they offered much more than he would ever be able to pay. What did they care about a father and a daughter? About taking a young girl from her family, her village, her home? For them, I was just something to buy and something to sell.

My mother was beyond understanding. Sobbing, she held me tight until the traders pulled me away. Away from my family, my village, my home.

It is hard to imagine, harder to remember. One moment I was doing my work as a pawn, waiting for the day when I would be back home, and the next moment, I was in a line of captives headed for the coast. There were men who had been snatched on their way to the rice fields, women who had been kidnapped right out of their houses at night, and children who had been pawned like me.

We walked for days and days, passing people going about
their lives as we had only days before: girls with calabashes full
of water on their heads, women washing in rivers, men work-
ing in fields, and boys climbing trees. Everyone and everything
made me think of home. Of my mother, my sisters and brothers, even my father. I cried myself to sleep thinking of them.

5

After many days, we came to the coast, to Lomboko.

"What are those strange people who look like ghosts?" I asked the others. They shrugged and spoke of magic and places far away.

Every day I woke thinking, *Today the ghosts are going to come and eat me. It will be today.*

SLAVE BARRACOON.

↑ *We were imprisoned in barracoons like this one.*

One day the ghosts did come for me, but not to eat.

Instead they brought us to the sea, a terrible moving blue thing I had never seen before.

6

I sobbed as we were pushed into the canoes, trembled when we came to the slave ship, and despaired as we boarded and went down into the dark hold.

And so I left Africa.

And so I left my home.

It took seven weeks.

Seven weeks in a dark and airless hold.

Seven weeks of heaving ocean.

Seven weeks of chains and shackles.

Seven weeks of sobs and cries.

IT WAS LATE AT NIGHT when we arrived in Cuba. Our captors gave us water and ordered us to clean ourselves. It felt extraordinary to bathe again. After weeks in filth, to be clean again was wonderful.

"Be quiet," we were warned. "Do not make a sound."

And so silently we came to that island, hundreds of us, in a dark so deep that we could barely see one another. The only sound was the wind in the trees. I felt invisible.

The next day, a white man bought four of us: a boy named Kale, two girls, named Kagne and Teme, and me.

We girls clung to each other while Kale walked ahead, following the white man through the streets of Havana. There were so many people, black and white, dressed in the strangest clothing we had ever seen. "How can they bear wearing so much?" I whispered to Teme. "It is as hot here as it is in Africa, where we wear so much less."

When a large, four-legged creature taller than a man clattered up behind us, we three girls jumped and screamed. This huge animal, pulling a cart full of goods, terrified us. Kagne, Teme, and I stumbled after Kale and the white man, trying to make sense of the smells, noises, and sights of this strange land.

Finally, we arrived at a wharf, boarded a ship we learned later was called the *Amistad*, and were sent down to the hold. Soon more captives joined us, all men and mostly Mende, like us. "What do these white men want with us?" I asked the others again and again. They shook their heads sorrowfully. No one knew.

Shortly after setting sail, we were summoned to the deck. Slowly, the men, shackled and chained together, made their way up the stairs; we children, who were not so encumbered, followed. There a man gave us each a banana and some water. One captive, later well known as Cinque, pointed to himself and then to all of us. "What is going to happen to us?" he asked. The man who had given us the food laughed, pointed to some barrels nearby, mimed throats being slit, then chopping, and then pointed again to the barrels.

They were going to eat us! There was now no doubt about it — they were planning to kill us for food! Back in the hold, Teme, Kagne, and I began to cry, but Cinque told us to stop. "Don't worry. I have a plan. Go to sleep," he said. Sleep? How could we sleep worrying that they might kill us? But we were so tired that we did. There was little wind, and the ship rocked so gently. Teme, Kagne, and I moved closer together, and before I knew it, I was asleep.

I dreamed of my mother.

Of her gentle hands when she plaited my hair.

Of her soothing words when I was vexed.

Of her comforting arms when I was afraid.

I dreamed of my mother.

I dreamed of home.

Once the ship was under way, both it and time seemed to crawl along. Hour after hour after hour, I sat in that dark hold. Hour after hour after hour, I imagined the worst. *Be done with it*, I thought. *If you want to eat me, kill me now.*

One night, I had almost nodded off when I heard Cinque whispering to the man next to me. Then there were some muffled clanking sounds, and the man stood up, rubbing his wrists. I could just make out in the darkness that his shackles were gone! I heard more murmurs and saw more men standing up. Cinque, it seemed, had found a nail and was able to free them all! I held my breath as they then searched the hold — what if the white men on deck heard them? But they were so quiet that if I had closed my eyes, I wouldn't have known they were moving at all. Then they found the knives, and I was able to breath again. "If we do nothing, we will be killed," whispered Cinque. "We may as well die trying to be free as to be killed and eaten."

There was a storm that night. When it was over, when everything was still, Cinque and the others attacked. Kagne, Teme, and I cowered together in the hold while the ship shuddered and shook. Above us were yells in Mende, screams in Spanish, splashing, cursing, and other even more dreadful sounds. Finally, it seemed to be over, and Kagne, Teme, and I crept up to the

deck. There was blood everywhere. White and African men lay
dead and dying. But we Africans had won; now it was the white
owners who were in chains! "Take us home." Cinque gestured to
them. "Sail this ship to Africa."

During the long days that followed, we children explored the ship. There was clothing, and Kagne, Teme, and I, remembering the overdressed people of Havana, tried it on, but without much success. Kale was much more interested in the various bits of leather, chasing after us with them, pretending to beat us.

"Come here!" I called to them after finding one magical object. "This is like water, but not! See? You can look into it and see yourself — just as if you were looking into a river." Kagne and Teme came over, looked, and then squealed and jumped back in alarm. Kale gingerly touched the object and then looked at me, surprised. "Yes," I told him. "It is completely dry. What on earth do they use it for, do you think?"

"Who knows?" he commented. "For that matter, what do you think they do with these?" "These" were sheets of paper all stuck together, with marks on them.

Since we Mende haven't a written language, we did not have any way of understanding what these were and soon put them aside. It was only much later that we learned of mirrors and books.

After days when we seemed to be making little progress, Cinque discovered that we were being deceived. Don Montez, one of the white owners, was sailing toward Africa during the day, but at night, he was using the stars to sail toward the shore, hoping that someone would see the ship and rescue him.

Home was now as far away as ever.

Finally, when our need for food and water had become desperate, we dropped anchor, and Cinque rowed to shore with a few others. Watching from the ship, I gasped when two white men came out of the woods and walked right up to Cinque, but I relaxed when I could see that they were friendly. Later we learned that one was a ship's captain and that Cinque had been negotiating with him to sail us home. Those of us on the ship were so engrossed in what was happening on shore that we didn't notice another ship drawing near. However, Cinque and the other men did. They yelled at us, jumped back into the boat, and began rowing back, but it was too late.

White men from the other ship poured onto ours. Don Ruiz and Montez ran to them and wailed and cried as they told their story, and it wasn't long before we were all prisoners again. Cinque had found out that we were in a part of America where slavery was illegal. But it seemed that he and the other men were to be tried for mutiny and murder. We children were needed as witnesses. All of us were to be held at the New Haven jail until the trial. Cinque worried about what would happen to us now. "We killed too many white men. Now they will hang us."

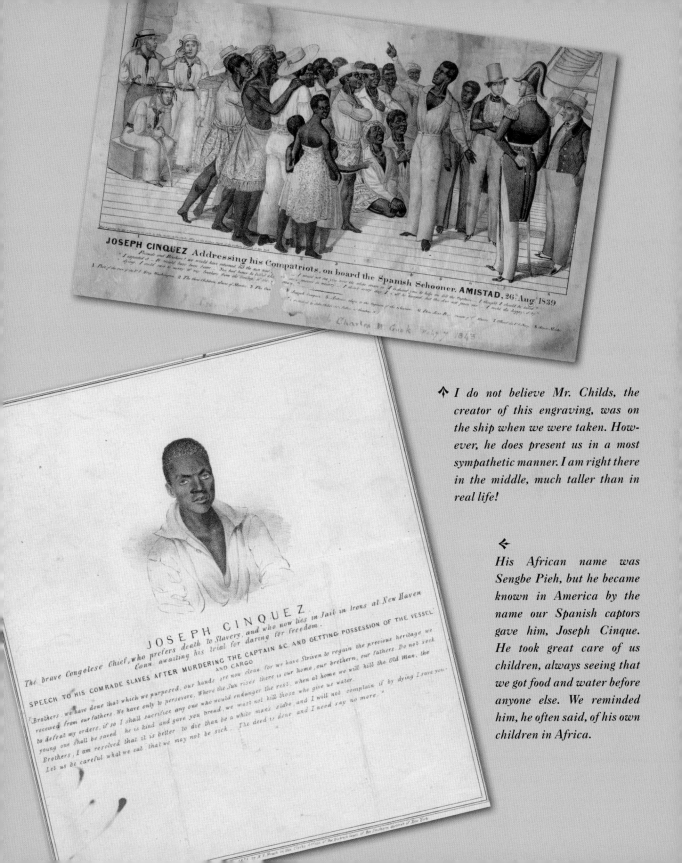

JOSEPH CINQUEZ Addressing his Compatriots, on board the Spanish Schooner. AMISTAD, 26ᵗʰ Aug 1839

JOSEPH CINQUEZ.
The brave Congolese Chief, who prefers death to Slavers, and who now lies in Jail in Irons at New Haven Conn awaiting his trial for daring for freedom.
SPEECH TO HIS COMRADE SLAVES AFTER MURDERING THE CAPTAIN &C. AND GETTING POSSESSION OF THE VESSEL AND CARGO

"Brothers, we have done that which we purposed, our hands are now clean for we have striven to regain the precious heritage we received from our fathers. We have only to persevere, Where the Sun rises there is our home, our brethren, our fathers. Do not seek to defeat my orders, if so I shall sacrifice any one who would endanger the rest, when at home we will kill the Old Man, the young one shall be saved, he is kind and gave you bread, we must not kill those who give us water.
Brothers, I am resolved that it is better to die than be a white man's slave and I will not complain if by dying I save you. Let us be careful what we eat that we may not be sick. The deed is done and I need say no more."

I do not believe Mr. Childs, the creator of this engraving, was on the ship when we were taken. However, he does present us in a most sympathetic manner. I am right there in the middle, much taller than in real life!

His African name was Sengbe Pieh, but he became known in America by the name our Spanish captors gave him, Joseph Cinque. He took great care of us children, always seeing that we got food and water before anyone else. We reminded him, he often said, of his own children in Africa.

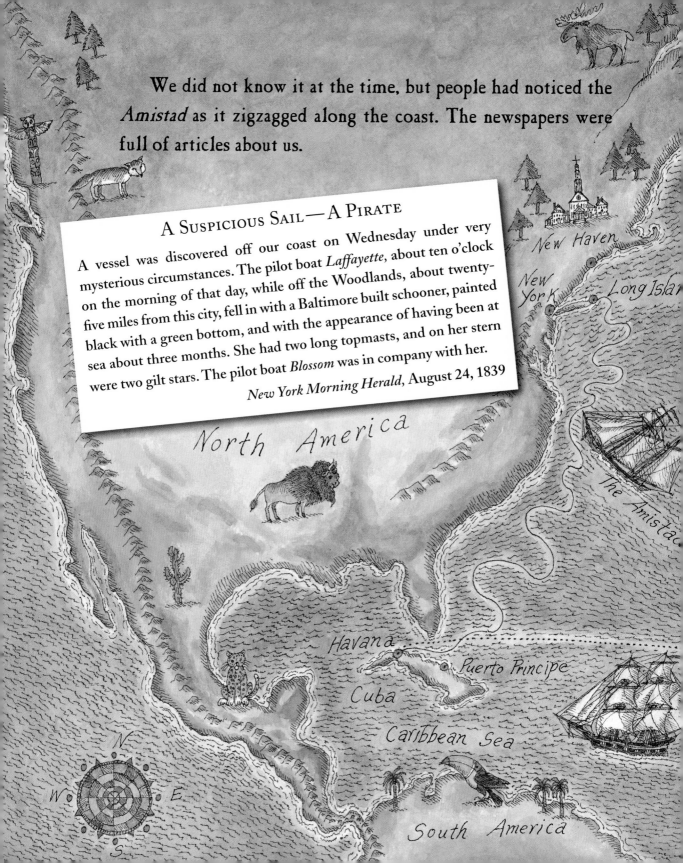

We did not know it at the time, but people had noticed the *Amistad* as it zigzagged along the coast. The newspapers were full of articles about us.

A Suspicious Sail — A Pirate

A vessel was discovered off our coast on Wednesday under very mysterious circumstances. The pilot boat *Laffayette*, about ten o'clock on the morning of that day, while off the Woodlands, about twenty-five miles from this city, fell in with a Baltimore built schooner, painted black with a green bottom, and with the appearance of having been at sea about three months. She had two long topmasts, and on her stern were two gilt stars. The pilot boat *Blossom* was in company with her.

New York Morning Herald, August 24, 1839

THE SLAVER — *Further particulars*

There was considerable excitement in the city throughout yesterday about the "suspicious vessel." She has been seen so often, and at each time manifested so much piratical feeling toward other vessels, that the people are beginning to get alarmed for the safety of their ships and friends. She was seen again last Saturday off Montague by the brig *Neptune,* and it is hoped that she has been captured ere this. If those on board had no intention at first of becoming pirates, farther than to liberate themselves from slavery, their necessities will compel them to resort to some rash act.

New York Morning Herald, August 28, 1839

THE LOW BLACK SCHOONER CAPTURED

The runaway schooner has been captured by the U.S. surveying brig *Washington,* Lieut. Gedney, and carried into New London. She is the "Armistad," of Puerto Principe, Cuba, and was owned by a Mr. Carrias, of that place. At the time she was taken possession of by the slaves, she was bound from Havana to Nouvitas, with a cargo of dry goods, and about fifty slaves. The slaves rose upon the captain and passengers, and killed nearly the whole of them.

The trial of these blacks will involve several curious questions, which we shall notice herafter.

New York Journal of Commerce, August 28, 1839

Atlantic Ocean

West Africa

Free Town

Mendeland

Lomboko

·········· Voyage from Africa to Cuba
———— Voyage of Amistad from Cuba
 to Long Island

ON LAND AT LAST, Kagne, Teme, and I stayed close together as we made our way through the streets of New Haven. The New Haven jail was just off the public square. The square was called a green, but it was certainly never as green as Africa! Like the streets of Havana, they were filled with strange people, strange sounds, strange smells, strange animals, strange buildings, and . . . strange . . . well, things we couldn't even identify, so strange were they to us. And how curious were the people! They stopped what they were doing to watch us go by, whispering and pointing. A group of children came right up to us, and one of them touched Kagne's hair before they all ran away, giggling and chattering loudly. It all seemed as far from my African home as the moon.

Mrs. Pendleton, the jailer's wife, brought us girls to a room away from the men and then pointed to a big pile of clothing on one of the beds. This was a complete puzzlement to us because, you see, girls in Mendeland wear very little, some cloth tied around the middle with perhaps a few beads. Cold as we were, much colder than we had ever been in our lives, the idea of putting on that clothing caused us to burst out laughing. Not for long, because Mrs. Pendleton made it clear that she was quite serious. We were to put that clothing on immediately.

Not wanting to anger this white lady, I grabbed a dress and tried to pull it over my head, but it wouldn't go. Mrs. Pendleton frowned, showed me that I had it upside down, and then turned her attention to Kagne, who seemed to have her dress on back to front. After much travail, we managed to get the dresses on correctly, and then Mrs. Pendleton showed us how to button each other. Finally she made us stand in a row and studied us. Frowning, she straightened a bit of cloth here, redid a button there. At last she seemed satisfied and left the room.

We stood in silence for a moment and then, at the very same time, all burst out laughing. Worried that Mrs. Pendleton would come back, we tried to stop, but all it took was one look and we started again. I laughed so hard, my sides hurt!

"These clothes look terrible and feel terrible," I said when I could speak again. "How can these people bear it? I can barely move! And look, there is still more on the bed!" I picked up a piece of cloth and wrapped it around my head.

"There, now I'm totally covered! I'm sure that white lady will be very pleased with me now!"

↑ *This is how I dressed as a child in Africa. Mende children wear much less than American children.*

↑ *And this is how I dressed as a child in America. So much more clothing!*

Mrs. Pendleton soon did come back, this time with a large group of people. Among them was Mr. Lewis Tappan, a man who became very important to all of us. He looked Kagne, Teme, and me up and down and then turned to those with him and talked with great enthusiasm. Knowing no English, we could not understand what he said; however, his gestures indicated that he was very much pleased with us. I couldn't help but smile when he turned back to us and eagerly greeted each of us in his language. Smiling and chattering away, he then bustled out, Mrs. Pendleton and the crowd following. "That man seems to be a very important chief," Kagne said. "I think he wants to help us."

Over the next few days, many people came to see us. The jail was packed with them. Later I learned that Mr. Pendleton was charging people to see us, saying it helped to pay for our expenses.

Cinque spent quite a bit of time with Mr. Tappan and, even though they did not speak the same language, agreed with Kagne that he wanted to help us. Still, Cinque was wary. "Don't tell them much," he warned us. "Be polite, be pleasant, but be careful." So we told them little but enjoyed ourselves nonetheless.

One such enjoyment was our first wagon ride. I must admit I was terrified when Mr. Pendleton started off and, in fact, more than a little tearful. For one thing, I wasn't sure where we were going, and for another, we had neither wagons nor horses in my homeland. However, I soon discovered that it was great fun and was quite sorry when it ended.

My, were people curious about us! Even before we could speak English, they tried through sign language and such to learn all they could about us. We taught one of our supporters, Mr. Gibbs, how to count to ten in Mende. He then went to the wharf and walked about, counting repeatedly, until someone recognized what he was saying. This was James Covey, originally from our country, who became our interpreter and helped Mr. Gibbs learn more about our language.

One evening, Mr. Tappan visited with some books. I had been so curious about the ones on the *Amistad,* so gladly stood next to him as he slowly turned the pages. "That is a goat!" I suddenly blurted out. He smiled at me, and together we studied the book's pictures.

I excitedly called Kagne and Teme over, and we went through the book again. Now we made animal sounds — hissing like snakes, bleating like goats, and chirping like birds. Kale came in, and we went through the book a third time. When Kale saw the leopard, he began slinking around like one and Mr. Tappan laughed.

More hopeful than I had been in some time, I looked at him and wondered, *Can this man, perhaps, help us get home?*

I dreamed of my father.

Of his happiness in good times, when rice was plentiful and our bellies were full.

Of his sadness in bad times, when there was nothing and I was taken away.

I dreamed of my father.

I dreamed of home.

Americans couldn't seem to get enough of us. Just days after we came, there was already a play about us at the Bowery Theatre. And Peale's Museum had an exhibition of wax figures supposedly cast directly from us.

Three weeks later, we were taken to Hartford for the trial. Certain that death awaited them at the end of this journey, the men had to be forced onto the canal boat, their faces grim. This certainly did nothing for my confidence, and so my face was puffy from crying by the time we arrived. The crowds at the Hartford jail were even greater than those in New Haven. Evidently Africans like ourselves were a novelty, and so people streamed into the jail, often traveling long distances, to see what we looked like.

⬆ *The Amistad men often entertained visitors to the jail with physical feats such as acrobatics and wrestling.*

Cuba, being part of Spain at this time, had laws that said that people born in Africa couldn't be sold as slaves, only those born in Cuba. One of our lawyers, Roger Baldwin, said to the judge:

> *"Here are these three children between the ages of seven and nine years, who are proved to be native Africans, who cannot speak our own language or the Spanish language, or any other but the language of their nativity. Does the honorable Court see they cannot be slaves? They were not born slaves, they were born in Africa."*

Our lawyers felt that Kagne, Teme, and I should not be prosecuted as we had nothing to do with the rebellion, and so, on the

first day of the trial, we were brought to the courtroom without the men. "Are they hanging Cinque and the others while we are here?" I whispered to Teme. All three of us cried and cried. Mr. Tappan tried to comfort us, but it was to no avail. It was only when we returned to the jail and found the men safe and sound that we started to feel better. The trial continued for many days, and the judge decided that, because the events on the *Amistad* had occurred outside the United States, the men would not be tried for murder or mutiny. Unfortunately, he did not also decide that we could go free; the laws and treaties regarding slavery were complicated, and so he scheduled another trial.

Back in New Haven, we girls were moved out of the jail to the nearby Pendleton home, where we helped with chores.

And most wonderful, there was a lovely surprise. Our supporters had set up a school in the jail for us with students from nearby Yale College as our teachers. By now we knew what those strange collections of paper we'd seen on the *Amistad* were — books, of course. And we further knew that the markings were writing. And now we were to learn to decipher them ourselves!

One of our supporters, Mr. Leavitt, wrote a schoolbook called *Easy Lessons in Reading for the Younger Classes in Common Schools*. I can no longer remember if it is the one we learned from, but I am sure it is very similar.

Mr. Leavitt opens with these instructions:

If you wish to know how to read well, you must learn these rules by heart.

1. Be careful to call your words right.

2. Learn to pronounce them properly.

3. Speak with a clear and distinct voice.

4. Do not read too fast. Read slow and carefully so as not to make any mistakes.

5. Be very particular to observe all the steps.

6. Learn to use proper emphasis and inflections of the voice. Ask your teacher to show you what that means and how to do it.

7. Endeavor to understand every word you read as you go along. Study our reading lessons very carefully before you read.

8. Try to read as if you were telling a story to your mother or talking to some of your playmates. Reading is talking from a book.

9. Take pains to read the poetry and not to sing it.

10. The emphatic words are printed in italic letters.

I loved going to school, where I was especially quick with numbers. But it was reading I wanted to learn most of all. I remembered the books Mr. Tappan had shown us when we first came — the ones with images of goats and leopards — and I was eager to read them on my own. Stories are what I craved most of all. For I missed terribly listening to the elders tell stories as we had every night in Africa, stories about animals, stories about our ancestors, all sorts of stories from which we learned how to be.

While in Africa we learned while sitting in the compound with our elders, in America we learned in a room with desks, pens, ink, books, and more. And how we studied — penmanship, geography, reading, recitation, writing, and arithmetic! I did well and enjoyed helping the others. When I dared to think about returning to Africa, I wondered what it would be like to teach Mende children how to read and write and do arithmetic. A school in Africa — imagine!

I dreamed of the elders.

Telling us children stories of greedy Spider and clever Rabbit.

Teaching us to be patient and brave always.

I dreamed of the elders.

I dreamed of home.

The next trial did not give us freedom, nor did the one after that; our case dragged on, and it seemed we would never make it home. The cold New England winter didn't help. The first snow was wonderful—we children jumped into snowbanks, threw

snowballs, built snowmen, went sledding, and had a glorious time. The second snow was great fun as well.

By the third, I was getting a bit tired of it, and by the fourth, I had had enough. "If I never saw another snowflake, I would be perfectly content," I grumbled to myself as I buttoned up my coat. Then I pulled on my gloves, wrapped my scarf around me tightly, shoved my bonnet snug onto my head, and tied my boots before trudging outside into that cold icy world. In Africa, even during rains, the most you ever need to stay warm is a light wrap.

One thing that kept me going was my new faith. Mr. Tappan early on had introduced us to the Scriptures and saw to it that we received spiritual instruction. Hearing such biblical stories as the trials of Moses and the Israelites or Daniel in the Lions' Den made me think of the stories of fortitude and goodness that the family elders had told me when I was small.

And I loved the religious services — the hymns, the sermons, the psalms, and prayers were so moving and beautiful. All of it gave me great solace during those many days of waiting, and a way of worshipping that would be part of me for the rest of my life.

A year and a half after we first arrived, our case finally came to the Supreme Court, far away in the country's capital, Washington, D.C. These judges for the most important court in the land would decide our fate once and for all. Fortunately Mr. Tappan had persuaded former president John Quincy Adams to argue our case. He was extraordinary, and on March 9, 1841, the court announced its decision: we had won. When we heard, we were beside ourselves with joy.

We cried, we sobbed, we danced, we sang with joy — at last we were free and going home to Africa! This is the last part of the Supreme Court decision. I only understand the part at the end where it says we are free!

> *Upon the whole, our opinion is, that the decree of the circuit court, affirming that of the district court, ought to be affirmed, except so far as it directs the negroes to be delivered to the president, to be transported to Africa, in pursuance of the act of the 3d of March 1819; and as to this, it ought to be reversed: and that the said negroes be declared to be free, and be dismissed from the custody of the court, and go without delay.*

To The Friends Of The African Captives,

The Committee have the high satisfaction of announcing that the Supreme Court of the United States have definitely decided that our long-imprisoned brethren who were taken in the schooner *Amistad*, ARE FREE on this soil, without condition or restraint. The opinion of the court was pronounced on Tuesday, March 9, by Judge Story.

In view of this great deliverance, in which the lives and liberties of thirty-six fellow-men are secured, as well as many fundamental principles of law, justice, and human rights established: the committee respectfully recommend that public thanks be given on the occasion, to Almighty God, in all the churches throughout the land.

S. S. Jocelyn.

Joshua Leavitt.

Lewis Tappan.

New York, March 11, 1841.

This is an announcement Mr. Tappan and the others put in the newspaper to tell of our freedom.

"Do you remember Africa?" I sometimes asked Kagne and Teme. Twelve years old now, I had been in America for almost two years. "I do," I said. "Being among people who look like us, eating rice and cassava, feeling the warm breezes — I remember it as if it was just last week. Imagine — no more white people asking us silly questions. No more oatmeal. No more snow and ice. I don't care how long it takes to get us back, I'll never forget my native land!"

It did take a while to get us back. Since the American government was not about to provide us with a ship to get us home, one would have to be hired and that cost money. In response to the announcement that we former *Amistad* captives would return to Africa to start a mission in Mende-land, donations began trickling in. The mission idea seemed wonderful to me; led by American missionaries, I would be able to share what I had learned about God with my Mende brothers and sisters.

While we were waiting for the committee to raise the necessary funds for the mission and our journey home, we needed a place to stay. Fortunately, a sympathetic group of people in Farmington, Connecticut, volunteered. Kale and the men moved there immediately, but a problem arose with Kagne, Teme, and me. We had been living with the New Haven jailer's family, the Pendletons, since shortly after our arrival, and they vehemently did not want us to leave. I now know that is because they used us as household servants, but at the time I thought it was because they genuinely cared for us. They were the only American family I had lived with and knew well, and so when they told us that they were the only ones who could protect us from being sold into slavery again, I believed them.

The Pendletons went to court to keep us with them, but the judge ruled that we should go to Farmington. Furious, the Pendletons increased their dire predictions.

"Do you really think they are going to help you get back to Africa? We doubt it very much. They don't care about you at all. We do."

By the day of our departure, I was in a complete state, which was only made worse when I walked outside. There I encountered a crowd of angry people, many I recognized as friends of the Pendletons, screaming at those who had come to take us to Farmington.

Without another thought, I ran. Looking back on it, I see that it was a silly thing to do. Where was I going to go, after all? They caught up with me before I was down the lane and dragged me, kicking and screaming, into the carriage.

And so my arrival in Farmington was far from auspicious. Fortunately, the Reverend Porter did not comment on my tearstained face. He and his family quickly made me feel at ease in their home. Teme and Kagne stayed with other families, who were equally kind and generous. Far from being sold into slavery, in Farmington I discovered what it was like to be free in America.

Kagne, Teme, and I saw each other every day; much of our time together was in school. I did so well that one of our new teachers, Mr. Raymond, said I might make a fine teacher at the mission. I also enjoyed attending Reverend Porter's Sabbath services, where, on one special day, I received a new name. While my parents had named me Magulu, which means "cherished" in our language, when I first came to America, I was misunderstood and called Margru, which they wrongly claimed meant "black snake." No Mende child would have been named for a

snake—we hate them! So what a relief it was to be rid of that dreadful name, which only reminded me of those early unhappy days in America, days I wanted to forget. Now that I was free, I wanted a free name as well—my new one, taken from the Scriptures, Sarah Kinson, was perfect.

To raise money for our journey home, Mr. Tappan took some of us on tour. We did these exhibitions, as he called them, in churches, meeting halls, theaters, and similar places.

The program would begin with one of our hosts leading us in an opening prayer. Then Mr. Tappan would talk about us. Next came Cinque, who would tell our story most dramatically, with gestures, shouts, and much moving about. The audience always applauded with great enthusiasm when he was done! Then we sang Mende songs and demonstrated our knowledge. Kale, for example, was an excellent speller and always impressed our audiences with his abilities in this area.

My part was to read aloud the 124th Psalm:

"If it had not been the LORD who was on our side —
let Israel now say —
if it had not been the LORD who was on our side,

when our enemies attacked us,

then they would have swallowed us up alive,

when their anger was kindled against us;

then the flood would have swept us away,

the torrent would have gone over us;

then over us would have gone the raging waters.

Blessed be the LORD,

who has not given us as prey to their teeth.

We have escaped like a bird from the

snare of the fowlers; the snare is broken, and we have escaped.

Our help is in the name of the LORD, who made heaven

and earth."

Some people were incredibly kind. When we visited a carpet factory in Lowell, the workers took up a collection for us.

Some people were incredibly unkind. In Hartford an innkeeper refused us rooms. Mr. Tappan pleaded with him to no avail. It was humiliating to stand on the wharf, and cold as well. Fortunately our supporters found families to take us for the night.

We finally left in November of 1841. On the day of our departure, Mr. Tappan and several others of our dearest friends traveled with us on a steamer out to our ship, the *Gentleman*. "Thank you, sirs, from the bottom of my heart for all that you have done for us," I said to them. Finally, after we said the Lord's Prayer together, they boarded the steamer and headed back to New York. I would miss them all; they had always been so good to us. And so I waved and waved, my eyes full of tears, until I could no longer see them. Then, taking a deep breath, I turned my face east. Toward Africa. Toward home.

The crossing was uneventful, but strikingly different from my previous one. Then I had been in a filthy dark hold, while this time I was in a pleasant cabin. Then I had little to eat, while this time I had all I needed. Then I barely moved, while this time I walked the deck every day. It was light instead of dark, heaven instead of hell, possibilities instead of dread.

After seven weeks at sea, I knew we were near Africa and I began studying the horizon for a sign of land. The others invited me to play games, to read, to sing, but all I wanted to do was watch for my homeland. When I first saw it, I thought my heart would leap out of my throat, but I stayed quiet until it was more evident, until I was sure, and then called out excitedly to the others. "Africa! Africa! Africa!" With that, all my fellow former captives rushed to the rail; when the dear details of our homeland began to emerge, so did our tears. With sobs and cries, we pointed things out to each other. "Look, over there! Palm trees — yes, palm trees!" "And see? A small house, is it not?" "And there, over there, a canoe!" "I don't believe it — I hear drums!"

By the time we arrived at the Freetown wharf, the scene was quite extraordinary. Somehow many Mende people had heard of our arrival and were singing and dancing as we came off the ship. I saw a man who looked so much like my father that it made me jump. However, a second glance made it clear that it was only wishful thinking. *No matter,* I thought, *Whether I see my father again or not, I'm home!*

After so many years in America, I was among my own people, among people who looked just like me, who spoke my native tongue. I saw women who looked like my mother, carrying babies on their backs just as she had; men who looked like my father, farmers ready to go out to their rice fields; and children who looked like my own brothers and sisters. I turned and smiled at Kagne and Teme; they were my sisters now.

There were wars in Mendeland, and so it took many months until the mission of Kaw Mendi was established on the island of Bonthe. Most of the *Amistad* men went back to their villages, but we children stayed at Kaw Mendi. I continued my studies with the hope that one day I would be a teacher at the mission school. Kagne, Teme, and I became closer than ever. It was a wonderful time for us.

Unfortunately, it was not a wonderful time for the Americans who were with us. After Mrs. Raymond lost a baby and became more and more distraught, Mr. Raymond decided she had to return to America. I was sent with her.

It was with very mixed feelings that I, now sixteen years old, once again crossed the ocean to America.

Mr. Tappan and Mr. Raymond felt that I should be properly trained as a teacher and so, instead of immediately sending me back home to Africa, they sent me to Oberlin College in Ohio.

It was a miserable time for me. I missed Africa terribly. "I would not stay in this country for a thousand dollars were it not for the education," I told a friend. On the worst days, the days when it was icy cold and nothing seemed right, I would creep up to my room and simply cry and cry and cry.

Everyone was very kind, but they did not understand. When I had been in America before, I had had Kagne and Teme with me. We had been through so much together and understood each other in ways no one else did. At Oberlin, no matter how kind and generous the friends I made were, not one was African. Not one had experienced what I had. They were not Kagne and Teme.

At last I did go home to Africa. For good. I became a teacher. I married. I was content.

Some days were trying, but others were so delightful that I wrote a friend, "My heart is filled with the love of God to do my people good."

Then came a day more joyous than any other.

The smallest girls were practicing their penmanship and the older ones their arithmetic. I stepped to the classroom doorway for a moment and looked out at the tall green palm trees reaching into the sky and the spreading mango tree in front of the school, all ready for a boy to climb. Looking up into the clear blue sky, with a few clouds coursing through it, I said a short prayer of thanks. After all I had been through, here I was, home in my beautiful country.

A slight sound to my side made me look around, expecting one of the little girls needing my help. But not at all: two men were standing there. "Magulu," one of them said softly. My Mende name. The name my father and mother gave me. A name I had not heard in years. "We come from your father," he continued. "Only the wars have kept him from coming himself. He wanted us to find out how you were. He wanted us to ask you if you forgive him."

I leaned against the doorway. "My father?" I said. "Keke? He is alive?" They nodded. "But of course I forgive him. He is my father. He did what he had to do at the time."

"This will make him happy." They smiled. "You will see him soon."

Now I was truly home.

I dreamed of Africa.

Of the people I loved and the country I admired.

I dreamed of Africa.

I dreamed of home.

AUTHOR'S NOTE

"Africa is my home. I long to be there. Although I am in America,
yet my heart is there. The people I love and the country I admire ..."
FROM A DECEMBER 18, 1847, LETTER BY SARAH WHILE SHE WAS AT OBERLIN

Children? There were children on the ship? It was the spring of 2000, and I was at an *Amistad* exhibit, of particular interest to me because the captives were from Sierra Leone, where I'd spent two years in the 1970s as a Peace Corps volunteer. Once I had learned about those children, I could not stop thinking about them. *What must it have been like for them?* I wondered. *What is their story?*

Before long, I honed in on Margru (the name by which she is known today) and sought out every reference about her while also broadening my knowledge of the *Amistad* affair, Sierra Leone at that time, and the slave trade. An early discovery was a collection of her transcribed letters during and after her time at Oberlin. Digging deeper, I came across newspaper articles, journals, maps, and engravings, as well as more letters and other remembrances from those who had known her and the other captives. Examining original material at Tulane University's *Amistad* Research Center was amazing — most of all, handling Margru's letters, with their faded yet still elegant handwriting. And when I retraced her steps in New Haven, Farmington, and Oberlin, it felt as if she were there, too.

Wanting to tell her story as truthfully as possible, I tried for years to write it as nonfiction. However, while she did forcefully express her feelings in letters as a young woman, there are no firsthand accounts from her as a child, and so I had to use phrases such as "Margru probably felt . . ." and "Perhaps she missed her parents." Finding this unduly awkward, I crossed the border to fiction, giving Margru a voice of her own. The story is still true; those instances where I have imagined her feelings, invented dialogue, or created scenes are based on my research and on firsthand experiences in Sierra Leone. For example, John Warner Barber, who interviewed her, wrote that she was "put in pawn by her father for a debt, which not being paid, she was sold into slavery." I researched pawning and, learning that it was often done in times of famine, invented that as the reason Margru's father pawned her. The final scene of Margru meeting emissaries of her father is something she mentioned in a letter. Whether they actually met we don't know. In fact, she and her husband left the mission not long after this and nothing further about her life is known.

I am very grateful to my family, friends, and those in the Dalton School community who supported me in a myriad of ways through the many years I worked on this project. Staff members at the *Amistad* Research Center, Mystic Seaport, the Oberlin College Archives, the Connecticut Historical Society, and the Farmington Library were all enormously helpful. A special shout-out goes to those who created Mystic Seaport's Exploring *Amistad* site, a trove of primary sources that is, unfortunately, no longer available. I am very appreciative of the help Marlene D. Merrill, Joseph Opala, and especially Konrad Tuchscherer, a specialist in African history and language, gave me. Most of all, I am beholden to Melanie Kroupa, who helped me shape the story; Karen Lotz, who decided she wanted it in an instant; editor extraordinaire Sarah Ketchersid; Robert Byrd, who illustrated Margru's story so beautifully; savvy designer Heather McGee; and my stalwart agent, Stephen Barbara.

꧁✤꧂

To the people of Sierra Leone
M. E.

To the memory of my mother and father
R. B.

SELECTED SOURCES

Abraham, Arthur. *The Amistad Revolt: An Historical Legacy of Sierra Leone and the United States.* Freetown, Sierra Leone: U.S. Information Service, 1987.

Barber, John W., comp. *A History of the Amistad Captives: Being a Circumstantial Account of the Capture of the Spanish Schooner Amistad, By the Africans on Board; Their Voyage, and Capture Near Long Island, New York; with Biographical Sketches of Each of the Surviving Africans; Also, an Account of the Trials Had on Their Case, Before the District and Circuit Courts of the United States, for the District of Connecticut.* New Haven, CT: E. L. & J. W. Barber, 1840.

Cable, Mary. *Black Odyssey: The Case of the Slave Ship Amistad.* New York: Viking, 1971.

Conneau, Theophilus. *A Slaver's Log Book, or 20 Years' Residence in Africa: The Original 1853 Manuscript.* Englewood Cliffs, NJ: Prentice-Hall, 1976.

Fyfe, Christopher. *A History of Sierra Leone.* London: Oxford University Press, 1962.

Lawson, Ellen NicKenzie, with Marlene D. Merrill. *The Three Sarahs: Documents of Antebellum Black College Women.* New York: Edwin Mellen Press, 1984.

Matthews, John, R. N. *A Voyage to the River Sierra-Leone, on the Coast of Africa.* London: B. White and Son and J. Sewell, 1788.

Sturge, Joseph. *A Visit to the United States in 1841.* Boston: Dexter S. King, 1842.

Thompson, George. *The Palm Land: West Africa Illustrated.* Cincinnati, OH: Moore, Wilstach, Keys, 1859.

———. *Thompson in Africa: An Account of the Missionary Labors, Sufferings, Travels, and Observations of George Thompson in Western Africa, at the Mendi Mission.* New York: printed for the author, 1857.

Winterbottom, Thomas. *An Account of the Native Africans in the Neighbourhood of Sierra Leone.* London: C. Whittingham and J. Hatchard, 1803.

IMAGE SOURCES

p. 19 (top): *Joseph Cinquez Addressing His Compatriots on Board the Spanish Schooner, Amistad* by John Childs, Chicago History Museum. p. 19 (bottom): *Joseph Cinquez,* Library of Congress, Prints & Photography Division, LC-B2-5289-11. p. 30 (top): "Long Low Black Schooner," TCS 65, Houghton Library, Harvard Theatre Collection, Harvard University. p. 30 (bottom): *The Amistad Captives,* Library of Congress, Prints & Photography Division, LC-USZ62-123182. p. 58: *Marqu* by William H. Townsend, Beinecke Rare Book and Manuscript Library, Yale University.

Text copyright © 2013 by Monica Edinger. Illustrations copyright © 2013 by Robert Byrd. All rights reserved. No part of this book may be reproduced, transmitted, or stored in an information retrieval system in any form or by any means, graphic, electronic, or mechanical, including photocopying, taping, and recording, without prior written permission from the publisher. First edition 2013. Library of Congress Catalog Card Number 2012947752. ISBN 978-0-7636-5038-4. This book was typeset in Caslon Antique. The illustrations were done in ink and watercolor. Candlewick Press, 99 Dover Street, Somerville, Massachusetts 02144. visit us at www.candlewick.com.

Printed in Dongguan, Guangdong, China. 13 14 15 16 17 18 TLF 10 9 8 7 6 5 4 3 2